SuicideWise
Taking Steps Against Teen Suicide

Nicole B. Sperekas

Enslow Publishers, Inc.

40 Industrial Road   PO Box 38
Box 398   Aldershot
Berkeley Heights, NJ 07922   Hants GU12 6BP
USA   UK

http://www.enslow.com

Library of Congress Cataloging-In-Publication Data

Sperekas, Nicole B.
    SuicideWise : taking steps against teen suicide / Nicole B. Sperekas.
        p. cm. — (Teen issues)
    Includes bibliographical references and index.
    Summary: Examines the causes and prevention of teenage suicide, sharing the
stories of some who survived and some who did not and providing warning signs
that may indicate if a friend is in danger of attempting suicide.
    ISBN 0-7660-1360-X
    1. Teenagers—Suicidal behavior, Juvenile literature. 2. Teenagers—Suicidal
behavior—Prevention, Juvenile literature. 3. Suicide—Juvenile literature.
4. Suicide—Prevention, Juvenile literature. [1. Suicide.] I. Title. II. Title:
SuicideWise. III. Series.
    HV6546.S65   2000
    362.28'0835—dc21   99-38534
                                                    CIP

Printed in the United States of America

10 9 8 7 6 5 4 3 2

To Our Readers: We have done our best to make sure all Internet addresses in this book
were active and appropriate when we went to press. However, the author and the
publisher have no control over and assume no liability for the material available on those
Internet sites or on other Web sites they may link to. Any comments or suggestions can
be sent by e-mail to comments@enslow.com or to the address on the back cover.

Illustration Credits: Courtesy of Joe and Julie Cunningham, p. 41; Courtesy of
Les Franklin, p. 42; Skjold Photos, pp. 10, 17, 29, 49.

Cover Illustration: Illustration by Harry Douglas; Background © Corel
Corporation.

Cover Description: Girl is comforting boy who has decided to discuss his
suicidal thoughts.

Contents

Acknowledgments

The author wishes to acknowledge the help of many people.

Les and Marianne Franklin—they shared the joys and sorrows concerning their son Shaka.

Joe and Julie Cunningham—for telling me about their son Jay and how their family coped as survivors of suicide.

Kelly—best friend of Ann.

Carol, mother of Micah—both best friends to John.

Stan, Sharon, and Debbie.

Doctors Lynn Levine, Holly Hedegaard, Lloyd Potter, Jim Selkin, and Arlene Metha.

Marcia Balogh, The Governor's Suicide Prevention Advisory Commission.

Reverend Vera Guebert–Steward and Carol Davis.

Mental Health Association of Colorado, especially Julie Underhill Butscher and Ed George.

Friends who read drafts of this book: Dr. Suzanne Kincaid, Max Price, Mary Williams, Francha Menhard, Ann Johnson, and Dr. Hannah Evans.

1

Overview of Suicide

I thought of suicide for a long time. I eventually tried to kill myself. I almost died.

Sharon, 15 (not her real name)[1]

Like Sharon, many teenagers have thought of suicide. Unlike Sharon, most teenagers do not ever go from thinking about suicide to actually making an attempt.

Suicide is the act of killing oneself. More than thirty thousand people of all ages commit suicide every year.[2] Nearly five thousand of these deaths are by young people between the ages of fifteen and twenty-four.[3] In fact, for this age group, suicide is the third highest cause of death after accidents and homicides.[4]

These figures are disturbing because the death of any young person is especially tragic and a cause for concern.

Experts agree that most people who commit suicide send warning signs first.[5] Most people who attempt suicide are ambivalent about whether they want to die. Their suicidal behavior is often, though not always, a cry for help. So, if teenagers can educate themselves about suicide, perhaps they can help prevent suicides—their own and those of their friends.

The number of teens who think about suicide or who make suicide attempts is much higher than the number of teens who commit suicide. When a suicide attempt results in death, it is called either a suicide or a completed suicide.

Suicide Attempts

It is impossible to know how many teenagers attempt suicide. No official numbers are kept.[6] Some numbers are provided by emergency rooms, police, coroners (medical examiners who determine the cause of death), and other

Facts to Know

- About 20 percent of high school students have thought seriously about attempting suicide in the past year.[7] This means that if a high school has 1,000 students, 200 of them have thought of attempting suicide.
- The rate of suicide is almost 11 suicides for every 100,000 teens ages fifteen to nineteen.[8]
- The completion rate for teen suicide is five times higher for males than for females.[9]
- The attempted suicide rate for high school females is more than twice as high as for males.[10]

sources. Many teenagers try to keep their suicide attempts a secret. Or they may tell a friend who does not report it. Thus, for every suicide attempt that is reported, there are many, many more that are not.[11]

Estimates of suicide attempts by young people vary: One estimate suggests that there may be as many as 250,000 to 500,000 attempts each year.[12] Even though the number of deaths from suicide is much lower than the number of attempts, the high attempt rate by teenagers is a serious concern. The attempt rate indicates the number of teenagers whose emotional pain and/or physical distress is so great that they see suicide as a way to escape their pain.

With every attempt, there is always the risk that teenagers may miscalculate either the dangerousness of their method and/or the likelihood that someone will save them. For example, a teenager may take some pills just to try to end his emotional pain, but unknowingly, takes enough to cause his death. This teenager may not really have wanted to die, but did.[13]

Suicide Deaths

The actual number of suicides each year is higher than the reported rate.[14] Many times, the cause of death is unclear. For example, the police or coroner may not be sure whether a death was caused by an accident or a suicide. Even crime scene experts cannot always tell for sure. When there is doubt, a coroner might list "accident" as the cause of death to protect the feelings of the family.[15] The following is an example of a death situation that police might question:

> Going at high speed, a teenager's car hit a tree. There were no passengers in the car and no other cars were involved. There were no skid marks. It is unclear

whether the teen had an accident (lost control or fell asleep) or deliberately killed himself.

Who Commits Suicide?

More men than women commit suicide.[16] This is true for teenage boys, too.[17] White males have the highest suicide rate.[18] Black females have the lowest.[19] However, the rate of black male suicide—ages fifteen to twenty-four—is increasing at a faster rate than for young white males.[20] Hispanic students are more likely than white students to make suicide attempts.[21] Certain American Indian tribes have high suicide rates.[22] The suicide attempt rates of gay youth are higher than those of heterosexual males.[23]

Many people question the reason for rising teenage suicide rates. It is not an easy question to answer. Many factors play a part, including

- Family breakdown and divorce[24]
- Increase in youth depressive disorders[25]
- Widespread availability and abuse of drugs and alcohol[26]
- Increase in pressures and stresses on teenagers[27]

Some people believe that the popular culture and media may contribute to the increase in teenage suicide rates. Although the results of a number of studies support this belief, conclusive evidence is lacking. Further research is needed.[28]

Copycat or Cluster Suicides

Cluster suicides occur when one or more people commit suicide in response to another person's suicide. This type of imitative suicide can occur from knowing the person personally. But cluster suicides can also occur in response

Rising Rates

The suicide rate for teens ages fifteen to nineteen has almost tripled in the last thirty-five years. The rate has gone from over three suicides per 100,000 teens (1960) to over ten per 100,000 (1995).

Rising Suicide Rates, Ages Fifteen to Nineteen, 1960–1995

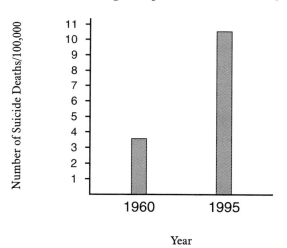

Year

Sources: National Center for Health Statistics—1960
Centers for Disease Control—1995

to suicides that are reported in newspapers, on television news, or in movies. Other "copycat" suicides occur when a famous person, such as a rock star, commits suicide, and as a result, some fans take their own lives.[29] When a student kills himself or herself, school staff members deploy specially trained counselors to help other students grieve

Most young people kill themselves by using firearms. Frequently, drugs and alcohol are also implicated in teen suicide.

and talk about the student's death.[30] This intervention is designed to reduce the possibility of suicide clusters.

How Teens Commit Suicide

Most young people kill themselves by using firearms.[31] Studies indicate that the risk of suicide is five times greater if guns are readily available.[32] The second most frequent method for male teenagers is hanging; for female teenagers, poisoning (especially overdosing with pills).[33]

Impulsive Versus Planned Suicide

Some teenagers begin thinking about taking their own lives and consider it for a long time. Then they begin making plans about how they will kill themselves. They choose the time, place, and method.

However, for other teenagers, suicide attempts are impulsive.[34] In this case, the teenager has perhaps thought of suicide for the first time. He chooses the method most available at that moment. It is more difficult to prevent impulsive acts, since the teenager may not give any warning signs. Teenagers are more likely than adults to make impulsive suicide attempts.[35]

Why Learn About Suicide?

The loss of any young person is tragic. Once teenagers learn about suicide, perhaps they can help themselves when in a crisis—or at least learn how and where to ask for help. Also, many teenagers know of other teenagers who are thinking about suicide or are sending warning signs. If more teenagers know about suicide, maybe they can help a friend who is at risk for attempting suicide.

2

Why Teens Commit Suicide

I felt that all my best friends had turned on me. I didn't fit in with them—they didn't let me in. And they said all sorts of things about me behind my back. Eventually they said things about me even when I was right there! It was like I was invisible.

Sharon[1]

Reasons for Suicide

Teenagers take their own lives for a number of reasons. People who study suicide use different methods to try to understand why people commit suicide. One approach is to study suicide notes people write before killing themselves. Since only about 15 percent of those who take their lives leave such notes, this method produces limited results. Sometimes the notes are written in such a disorganized and distorted fashion that researchers reading them remain unclear about the true motive or motives. Some notes reflect the mind-set of the writers, often dominated by negative emotions. Other notes contain certain themes or emotions common to young people who commit suicide, such as romantic breakups, difficulties with parents, or serious depression.[2]

Another approach is to interview teens who have attempted suicide to learn why they tried to kill themselves. Sometimes only one reason is given; sometimes many reasons are given. Sometimes the reasons are not clear—just vague feelings about wanting to end the emotional pain they feel. Others talk about a difficult situation they are facing and not knowing how to cope. They begin to feel hopeless and helpless about their ability to bring about any change. Most who attempt suicide say afterward that they really did not want to die. Their suicide attempt was the only solution they could come up with to end some pain or to cope with a problem that seemed unsolvable. They were so upset about their situation they were unable to see any options besides killing themselves.

Once the idea of suicide enters the person's mind, he or she may think about suicide from time to time. Sometimes, he or she also may be thinking about it seriously. At another minute or another day, he or she may be feeling better and decide that suicide is not the answer. The teen swings back and forth between being suicidal and not being suicidal. This inner struggle may go on for a long time and can wear the person down emotionally and physically. During this inner struggle, the person usually looks for something to tip the scale in favor of living. This is when a good friend can help by showing he or she cares.

The most common factors that lead to youth suicide are depression, social isolation or not fitting in, family disturbance or breakdown, drug and alcohol abuse, and low self-esteem. In many cases, more than one of these reasons is present.

Depression: A Common Cause of Suicide

Studies of suicide suggest that psychiatric disorders play a part in most teen suicides. The most common of these emotional illnesses is depression. More than 40 percent of adolescents who killed themselves suffered from a major depression—a depression that has a number of symptoms and lasts two or more weeks.[3] Some researchers believe the percentage of suicides caused by depression is higher than that.

Most people occasionally experience some "down" times or feelings. These temporary feelings of emotional distress are not really depression. Depression is a medical illness with specific signs and symptoms, not a temporary low moment in mood. Teenagers who have made suicide attempts often describe symptoms of depression such as periods of sadness or crying, fatigue, changes in appetite and sleep, irritability, and hopelessness. Their sense of hopelessness may cause them to believe that there are no solutions to their situation or problems.[4]

Depression can also lead to distortions in perception and thinking that can intensify a teen's suicidal thoughts. These distortions may result in the perception that his or her present crisis has gone on forever, as well as faulty interpretations and overreactions to certain events.[5]

What Causes Depression?

Depression is associated with changes in the chemistry of the brain. Usually, there is an imbalance of neurotransmitters (chemicals that help transport nerve impulses in the brain).[6] This type of brain chemistry imbalance is sometimes inherited, but not always. In addition to changes in brain chemistry, depression is also associated with difficult life situations or problems.[7] Some of these situations could include the death of a parent or close friend, rejection by friends or romantic breakup, feeling victimized, feeling ashamed about certain behavior, chronic health problems, family problems, failure in school or in other important areas of a teen's life. Most teens, however, do not become depressed when they face these problems.

Common Signs of Depression

- Feelings of sadness or irritability and personality changes that last for more than two weeks
- Loss of interest in everyday activities; boredom with self and others; withdrawal from others
- Difficulty making decisions or concentrating
- Eating all the time or having no interest in food
- Trouble sleeping or sleeping too much
- Tiredness or lack of energy most of the time
- Feelings of hopelessness, guilt, or worthlessness that last for more than two weeks
- Physical restlessness or the feeling of being slowed down
- Persistent suicidal thoughts[8]

Some teenagers react to their depression in ways not typically associated with depression. For example, it is not uncommon for depressed teens to be defiant and to act out in rebellious and aggressive ways.[9]

Treatment for Depression

The risk of suicide is higher if a person is depressed. Fortunately, depression usually can be treated by medications and by therapy with a counselor. So it is important to know the signs of depression and to get help.

Social Isolation or Not Fitting In

Another common cause of suicide among young people is social isolation or the feeling of not fitting in. Rejection by two good friends began Sharon's downward spiral toward thinking of suicide.

Being popular and having lots of friends is a big pressure in adolescence. Everyone wants to have friends and be liked. When friends start rejecting other teens and spreading rumors, it is easy to become upset.

Other teenagers feel that they have never fit in with other young people. Maybe they have poor social skills. Or maybe they are poor and do not wear the "in" clothes. Some teenagers have physical or emotional problems that cause other teens to stay away from them. In spite of wanting to fit in and be like others, these teens are rarely accepted and live their lives feeling very lonely and rejected. Some may become very angry and act out their anger by hurting others. Some teens may turn their anger inward and begin thinking of suicide.

Family Disturbance or Breakdown

Some teenagers have troubled families. The father or mother may be abusive—emotionally, verbally, sexually, or physically. One of the parents may be in trouble with the law. A parent may have some serious emotional problems that make it difficult for that parent to be a good, nurturing parent. A brother or sister may be causing problems in the

The risk of suicide is higher if a person is depressed. Fortunately, depression can be treated with medication and therapy.

A Talk With Sharon

When Sharon was fourteen, she took a number of painkillers prescribed to her for a painful arm condition in order to kill herself. She had lost consciousness by the time her mother came home from work. Her mother called 911, and Sharon was rushed to the hospital. The paramedics had to work very hard to keep her alive, giving her cardiopulmonary resuscitation and medications to restore her breathing. She almost died. Sharon tells her story:

I had introduced two of my best friends to each other. At first, the three of us did everything together. A little later the two of them became best friends and began to exclude me. They began to say things about me to other kids that weren't true. They said that I did drugs, drank, and was a whore.... I would make a new friend at school. Before I knew it, one of these "friends" would get to this new friend and before long, he or she would start avoiding me.

I tried to talk to the girls. They just ignored me. I felt like nothing I did helped stop them from spreading rumors about me. I began to cry a lot at home. I hid what was happening from my family. I began to get depressed.

There was no one to talk to. My two best friends had betrayed me.... A few kids were still my friends but I didn't want to burden them. Besides, my style was to keep everything inside and put on a happy face.

I thought I could pull out of this myself. But I got more and more depressed and I was in a lot of pain from my arm. Soon, I began thinking about suicide. I didn't think I'd ever do it because I was too chicken. But more and more, I just couldn't see any way out of the mess I was in.

I don't think I really wanted to die but I definitely wanted my life to change. I felt awful.

I began to think about suicide a lot. Not all the time. I'd flip-flop every day. If someone was nice to me in school, I'd start thinking that maybe I'd be okay. Sometimes I'd think about how much it would hurt my parents and sister if I killed myself. Then I'd stop thinking about it for a while. I'd write pros and cons about killing myself in my diary. I thought my situation was like torture. That was one of the reasons I listed to kill myself—to end the torture.[10]

home by his or her behavior. There may be constant arguing or conflict. Some of these problems go on year after year, and can be quite harmful and painful to all family members.

Many teenagers have to deal with the divorce of their parents. Divorce is very difficult for most children and teens. If the parents seemed happy before a divorce, the split can be a shock to the children. During the divorce, and after, the parents often put children in the middle of their conflict and pressure them to take sides. These tensions are very difficult for children and teenagers to handle.

Even if the parents are friendly and cooperative during and after a divorce, children and teens still may experience feelings of loss. They may not see one parent as often. Their lifestyles change and there may be less money to meet the family's needs. Some children may feel guilty about the divorce and worry that it was their fault. It is possible that some children will become depressed as the result of their parents' divorce.

Drug and Alcohol Abuse

Drug and alcohol abuse are associated with suicide. For example, over 50 percent of teens who killed themselves had a substance abuse problem.[11] There are several ways that drug and alcohol abuse may cause a teen to attempt suicide. Some teens are depressed and abuse drugs or alcohol as a way to self-medicate. They use drugs and alcohol to decrease their depression and feel better. Unfortunately, alcohol and many drugs are "downers." They may help a person feel better for a short time, but eventually, the teen ends up feeling more depressed.

Other teenagers take drugs and/or alcohol, not because they are depressed, but to help fit in or perhaps to rebel against parents. After a period of continued abuse, the alcohol and drugs may cause depression.

While under the influence of drugs and alcohol, some people become self-destructive. They act impulsively and engage in dangerous behavior. So there is an increased risk of suicide or accidental death due to drugs and alcohol.

If a teenager is already somewhat suicidal, abusing drugs and alcohol greatly increases the risk of suicide by removing any inhibitions the person has to kill himself or herself.

The Danger of Drugs and Alcohol

Stan is twenty and in college, studying psychology. When he was a teen, he abused drugs and alcohol. Between the ages of sixteen and eighteen, he made numerous attempts to kill himself.

I was always a quiet person and sort of uneasy with friends. I began drinking to help me be accepted. I found out that drinking also helped me feel more comfortable with others. I talked a little more and was less inhibited. Soon I began to drink more. Then I began using drugs and I got very depressed. I felt totally cut off from my parents. They tried to help and understand me, but I always felt they liked my older brother better—he was real outgoing, doing well in school, and had lots of friends.

Soon I was really boozing it up and getting drunk a lot. Then I got the idea to just go as fast as possible when I was driving alone out in the country. I sort of wanted to die but not really. I was okay with the idea of dying and was okay if I didn't die. Several times I was really out of control and drove over a hundred [mph]. I remember being surprised I was still alive after some of these wild rides. I got into several accidents but the police weren't called so I escaped [without] getting my license taken away. One time I got really sick from the alcohol and drugs and ended up in the hospital. At that point my parents realized I had problems. I finally got some help for my substance abuse. Finally, I stopped doing drugs and alcohol. Looking back on those two or three years, I almost died at least five or six times.[12]

Treatment for Drugs and Alcohol

Fortunately, substance abuse is treatable. There are many different types of programs designed to help teenagers with drug and/or alcohol problems. Alcoholics Anonymous (AA), Narcotics Anonymous (NA), as well as programs run by hospitals or mental health clinics offer special treatment programs and approaches for teenagers who abuse drugs or alcohol.

Low Self-Esteem

Some teenagers struggle with low self-esteem, feelings of worthlessness, or a low opinion of themselves. For whatever reason or reasons, they do not feel confident, and they can easily become humiliated and embarrassed, or can feel as if they are failures. Low self-esteem causes them to be vulnerable to depression, drugs and alcohol, isolation, poor school performance, or acting out. The normal problems and stresses of the teenage years are particularly difficult for teenagers to handle when they have low self-esteem. Thus, their low self-esteem and the sense of failure they feel may cause them to attempt suicide.[13]

Low self-esteem usually begins early in life. Some families are not very strong or nurturing. Some teens who have had learning, physical, or emotional difficulties may experience low self-esteem. Children and teens who have experienced any form of abuse may never feel good about themselves. Identifying teens with low self-esteem is not always easy. Many teens with low self-esteem have learned to cover up negative feelings about themselves and outwardly can look happy and confident.

Suicide Trigger Events

Many teenagers are depressed and do not attempt suicide. This is true, also, of teenagers who feel they do not fit in, have some kind of family breakdown, use drugs and alcohol, or have low self-esteem. What finally happens to push a teenager either to attempt suicide impulsively or to make a plan to commit suicide and carry out the plan? Often an incident occurs that adds more pain to an already existing painful situation or condition (depression, social isolation or not fitting in, family breakdown or divorce, drug and alcohol abuse, or low self-esteem). This trigger event (crisis) can lead to suicidal thoughts and behavior. What are some of the more common trigger events?

- Failure to make a team
- Argument with a parent; a disciplinary crisis with parents or school
- Breakup with a boyfriend or girlfriend
- Trouble with the law or being sent to jail or juvenile detention
- Failure to get into a school or college
- Death or suicide of a parent, relative, or close friend
- School failure; failing an important exam[14]

Any trigger event can cause a teenager to attempt suicide, but most often one or more of the common causes of suicide is already present.

For example, a teenager may be very depressed, but has never thought about suicide. Then, this teenager's girlfriend breaks up with him. The breakup is the trigger event, and he begins to think about suicide and then makes an attempt. Another teenager feels picked on and rejected by other teenagers, though there is one boy who likes her. She gets into an argument with her parent about going on a date with this boy. The argument gets ugly, and she feels rejected by her peers and her parent. She is angry and very unhappy and makes a suicide attempt.

Risk Factors

Risk factors are feelings, behavior, or situations that increase the risk of suicide. This does not mean that if one or more risk factors is present, a teenager will try to commit suicide. It means that, compared with a teen who does not have one or more of the risk factors, a teen with risk factors is at a higher risk of suicide.

Risk Factors of Suicide

- Prior suicide attempts or family history of suicidal behavior
- Depression or family history of depression
- Drug or alcohol abuse
- Poor school performance
- Isolation; withdrawal from others; alienation
- History of sexual or physical abuse
- Family conflict or divorce; death in family
- Poor coping or problem-solving skills
- Trigger event or life crisis[15]

Many teenagers have one or more of these risk factors, and they struggle with some of the common causes of suicide (such as depression or family breakdown), yet they never think about suicide. Others think about it occasionally but never seriously consider suicide and never make an attempt. Why is this? What do the majority of teenagers have that enables them to cope with most of the pressures of everyday life?

Studies suggest that teenagers who have a strong relationship with a parent and who feel connected to other teenagers are less likely to attempt suicide. If they feel a part of things and seem to be doing well in school, there is less risk that they will develop suicidal thoughts. Strong values or religious faith help protect against suicide.[16] Other protective factors against suicide or a suicide attempt include a strong sense of self-worth, good decision-making skills, and the ability to cope with stress.[17]

3

Helping a Suicidal Friend

I wished a friend would have noticed how upset and depressed I was getting. Maybe I wouldn't have slipped so deeply into a black hole. If you see a friend in trouble, say something, do something. Just don't stand there.

Debbie, made a suicide attempt at age 18[1]

Many teenagers know other teens who have thought of suicide or who have attempted suicide. In fact, a recent poll found that 46 percent of all teens said they knew someone who had tried to commit suicide.[2] Since suicidal thoughts or attempts may occur frequently, it is very important to be able to recognize the signs of suicidal thought or planned suicidal behavior. Familiarity with these warning signs of suicidal thought or behavior is perhaps the best hope of preventing a possible suicide.

Warning Signs of Suicide

Most people who think about suicide or who seriously plan their suicide give warning signs.[3] They are not sure they want to die, but they need help and are either in a lot of emotional pain or in a situation they consider hopeless. They want the pain or the situation to go away.[4]

Some teens express warning signs directly; others express warning signs indirectly. Often, people considering suicide have tried to think of solutions but for various reasons, only one comes to mind—to take their life. People who are depressed or using drugs or alcohol often think negatively. They feel so hopeless about their situation it is especially difficult to see a positive solution to their problems.[5] Others have struggled with family breakdown or other problems for so long that they, too, cannot see any positive choice that will make the situation or pain more bearable.

What are the common warning signs that indicate a teenager might be thinking about or planning his or her suicide?

Talking about suicide. Talking about suicide or making suicidal threats should be taken seriously. Some think that if a person talks about suicide, he or she will not act. This assumption is mistaken. Over 80 percent of teenagers who commit suicide talked about their suicidal ideas or feelings before they took their lives. Of those, only half confided in a peer or sibling.[6]

Making statements about how life is hopeless or that he or she is worthless. When a person makes these kind of statements, suicidal thought is common.

Giving away a favorite or prized possession. A teen who gives a friend a favorite CD or baseball glove may be making plans to commit suicide.

Engaging in risky behaviors or an increase in accidents. Driving fast while drinking or using drugs or mixing drugs and alcohol may be clues that the person does not care if he or she gets hurt or dies.

Any drug or alcohol abuse. Since drug or alcohol abuse increases the risk of suicide, any drug or alcohol abuse should be viewed as a possible warning sign of suicide.

Extreme moodiness, depression, or sadness. Moodiness, being "down" all the time, crying, a mood of irritability, hopelessness, or continual sadness may signal depression and suicidal risk.

Any change in sleep or appetite patterns. When a person begins to have difficulty sleeping or sleeps all the time, or when a person is either eating all the time or never hungry, he or she may be at risk.

Changes in behavior or personality. Any significant change in a person's usual behavior or personality is a warning sign of suicide. For example, a teenager who once was outgoing and always with friends now stays home and resists spending time with friends. Or perhaps a teenager who was once very personable and friendly is now angry, sullen, or aggressive. A teenager who was a good student begins to fail classes or a teenager who had lots of interests and was involved in many activities is no longer interested in anything.

Any change in a person's health or an increase in physical complaints. A person who suffers a major injury or illness may become depressed and suicidal. A person who begins to have numerous physical complaints may develop depression.[7]

When There Are No Warning Signs

Unfortunately, since teenagers often commit suicide impulsively, there are instances when they do not give warning signs.

It Came Out of the Blue

Jay was eighteen when he took his life. He was a senior in high school and had been admitted to college. He was going to study engineering. His parents, Joe and Julie Cunningham, talked about Jay's death.

> Jay was just a few weeks from graduating. He got good grades and enjoyed playing baseball and soccer. He had lots of friends. He was excited about going to college. As far as we know, he didn't do drugs or alcohol. We were a very close family. He was very sensitive, always upbeat, and had a great sense of humor. There were no signs of depression. That night he was studying calculus with a friend. After his friend went home, he said good night to us and went to bed. He spoke on the phone with his girlfriend. Shortly after that, he shot himself with a shotgun. We were asleep but something woke up Julie. Days later we realized that what she heard was probably the shotgun going off. Julie found him in his room the next morning when his alarm kept going off. His retainer was still in his mouth. After his death, we tried to ask everyone who knew Jay if they had noticed any suicidal signs. There were none. Our best guess is that something was said in that last phone conversation with his girlfriend that devastated him and he impulsively shot himself.[8]

How to Help Others

Sometimes a teen shows one or more of the warning signs of suicide. Knowledge of the warning signs of suicide as well as the risk factors can help a friend evaluate how serious the situation may be. For example, if a teen makes suicide threats (a warning sign) and has previously made a

Knowledge of the warning signs of suicide can help a friend evaluate how serious the situation may be. Be direct if you suspect a friend is suicidal; ask if the person is thinking of taking his or her life.

suicide attempt (a risk factor), a friend should be alarmed. The more warning signs and the more risk factors, the more serious the risk of suicide. But even if a teen displays only one warning sign, the possibility of suicide should not be ignored.

What should a teen do who suspects a friend or acquaintance may be thinking about suicide or when one or more warning signs are present?

It is best to be direct. Ask the person if he or she is thinking of suicide. Do not be put off by a "No" answer. It is common for suicidal teens to deny their suicidal thoughts.

Express concern. Tell him or her of any warning signs

that have been observed. The teen may be embarrassed about his or her suicidal thoughts and may resist talking about them at first. Reassure the teen that he or she is not crazy. Show him or her that just talking about suicide need not be scary.

Listen with care and concern. Let him or her talk about these suicidal thoughts. Let the person know that he or she will not be rejected for having these thoughts. Do not be judgmental. Mainly, listen. Allow the teen to express feelings and accept those feelings. Once a friend begins to talk about suicide, ask the person if he or she has made any plans and chosen a method.

Do not make light of suicidal feelings. Take suicidal thoughts or feelings seriously. Do not minimize these feelings. Do not dare the suicidal person by making remarks such as: "Oh, you're too chicken to do that," or "I bet you'd never do that."

Offer hope and possible solutions. Suggest that most problems can be solved. Do not hint that there are quick or easy solutions.

Seek Adult Help

If a friend is seriously considering suicide, seek adult help. It is difficult to go through this alone. Do not be sworn to secrecy. A friend's life may be on the line. Better to lose a friendship (by not keeping his or her suicidal thoughts or plans a secret) than lose the friend to suicide. Seek adult support. An adult will often know some resources or how to obtain further help.

Call a suicide help line or hot line and stay on the scene while the teen talks to a counselor. Or take the person to a suicide crisis center. Counselors there are trained to help teens make the decision not to take their own lives. They will stay on the line or speak with the teen as long as it takes to work through the crisis and reduce suicidal thoughts. Do not leave the suicidal person alone. Continued presence reassures the teen that he or she is cared for and is not going to be abandoned. Stay with the teen until it is clear that he or she will be safe. Another action can include removing available means to suicide, such as pills or guns.

Other possible resources are emergency rooms of hospitals, mental health clinics, clergy, youth counselors, and counselors at school.[9]

Teenagers with a suicidal friend should realize that even if they try to help their friend, there is still a risk that the friend will commit suicide. Doing everything one can and doing one's best may not be enough if a friend is determined to die.

4

Surviving Suicide

It hurts. I will never be the same person I was before Shaka's suicide.

Les Franklin, Shaka's father[1]

What Is a Survivor?

After a person commits suicide, many people close to that person are left to deal with the death. Family members, close friends, and acquaintances of the dead person are called survivors. Survivors find recovering from the suicide of a loved one particularly difficult. For most deaths, the cause and the reason are known. If a person dies by natural causes, an accident, or a homicide, the cause and the reason are identified. But a survivor of a death by suicide rarely, if ever, knows the reason the loved one committed suicide. For the rest of their lives, most survivors struggle with the reason that their son, sister, or close friend killed himself or herself.

Everyone grieves differently over the death of a person close to him or her. There is no one way or right way to grieve. Even so, there are some common features of grieving.

Shock and Disbelief

The sudden and unexpected death of a young family member or a close friend is almost always a shock. People do not want to believe that the person is really dead. They want to think that they are imagining or dreaming this. When they wake up, they will realize it was a nightmare. They think that at any moment someone will tell them that this is not really happening.[2]

Many survivors experience numbness and feel as if they are on "automatic pilot." They get to the end of the day but cannot remember anything they did or felt during the day. They know they got up in the morning, got dressed, ate, made phone calls, spoke with other family members and friends. They just do not remember doing any of that.[3]

Other survivors find themselves overwhelmed with emotions, especially sadness. They may cry uncontrollably. Or they may feel like crying but cannot.[4]

Many Faces of Anger

Survivors often find themselves feeling very angry. They feel their anger directed toward different people, including themselves.

Anger at the person who committed suicide. Some of the thoughts experienced by survivors are the following: What a stupid thing to do. He had so much to live for. He did not think about us—our pain and how we are going to go on without him.[5] Survivors are often filled with rage and anger at the person who committed suicide.[6] They may feel angry for years.

Anger at themselves. Survivors often direct anger at themselves. They may feel that they could have prevented the death. They think about all the times they had with the dead person. They wonder whether the person might not have committed suicide if they had spent more time with him or her, listened more carefully, or showed more love and affection.[7]

Anger at others. Survivors may feel that other people close to the dead teenager may be responsible for the teen's death. A teen may have told a close friend that his parent did not understand him. This close friend may feel angry with the parent, feeling that the friend's suicide was the parent's fault. Maybe a coach criticized a teen's performance at practice and shortly afterward, the teen committed suicide. A survivor may feel angry at the coach, blaming him or her for the teen's death.

When something happens that is out of our control, it is easy to feel angry. We want to find fault, to blame someone.[8] If we can find someone else to blame, we reduce our own sense of grief and guilt. For this reason, suicide can trigger intense feelings of anger.

Feeling Guilty

Survivors usually think about everything that happened before the teenager committed suicide. They wonder if they missed something. Maybe they overlooked a warning sign. Maybe they did not ask the person how he or she was feeling or if the person needed help. Survivors feel that in some way they let the teenager down. Parents, especially, feel guilty. They review how they treated their son or daughter and can easily find a way to blame themselves. Of course, survivors can never know for sure if something they did may have caused or triggered the suicide. Their guilt may last a long time.[9]

Intense Grief

Intense grief may include anger and guilt. Grief usually involves some depression and sadness. The survivor is very aware of a great loss. Survivors feel emotional, and sometimes physical, pain. Their pain is so great that they sometimes make a connection between the pain they are suffering and the pain the teenager may have suffered before committing suicide. Sometimes the survivor finds this helpful—a way to understand a little better why the teenager took his or her life. Intense grief can cause survivors to have their own symptoms of depression. They may find it difficult to sleep or may lose their appetite, stop eating, and lose weight. It is difficult for them to concentrate and their memory is poor. They are tired all the time.[10]

The grief of some survivors is so great that they may find themselves having suicidal thoughts. They do not know how they are going to go on without the loved one. They do not want to go on living.[11]

I Think About Her Every Day

Kelly (not her real name), age seventeen, is a survivor. Her best friend, Ann, committed suicide several years ago.

> Ann was very depressed. She talked to me about suicide. I didn't take this very seriously, though I was concerned. I don't know if anything I could have done might have saved her but I don't think I did enough. I've been depressed ever since. I miss her. Sometimes I pretend she's here and I yell at her for what she did. Sometimes

I'm angry at me—for doing too little. Mostly, I'm just down.[12]

The Difficulties of Grieving

Survivors find grieving after a suicide particularly difficult and complicated.[13] Suicide triggers strong emotions. A number of factors make grieving after a suicide more difficult than grieving after other kinds of deaths.

Suicide is not as common as other causes of death. Many people have experienced the death of an older person or the death of someone who had a long illness. Deaths caused by accidents are common; deaths by suicide are not common. Most people have not attended a funeral of a young person who has taken his or her life. Dealing with death is sometimes uncomfortable, and dealing with a teenager's suicide is especially uncomfortable and painful.

Death by suicide is not understood. Most people find it difficult to understand why a young person would take his or her life. Some people find the idea so strange that they make judgments about the person or the family members of that person. They may say that the dead teenager must have been crazy, or that his or her parents are responsible in some way for the death of their child.[14] Family members of the teenager may feel some shame. They may believe the suicide was their fault or that other people blame them for the teenager's death. Rumors and gossip sometimes get back to the grieving family members, only to add to their pain and loss.

Survivors of suicide have to deal with the strong emotions of suicide—particularly anger and guilt. These two emotions make grieving more difficult and complicated.

The death of a teenager by suicide leaves most survivors with a puzzle: Why? Since the dead teenager cannot tell the survivors why he or she did this, survivors try to solve the puzzle themselves. This is very hard to do. Survivors find themselves thinking about this question almost all the time.[15] The suicide is a mystery survivors try to solve. They find any reason they come up with unsatisfactory, since they can never know for sure if the reason is the correct one.

Still Grieving

John (not his real name) was eighteen at the time of his death. He committed suicide in 1990. He had graduated from high school and had been an average student. From grade school until his death, his best friend was Micah. He would spend lots of time with Micah at Micah's home. He really liked Micah's parents and sister. He felt as if he was a part of the family. Micah's family would take John with them on vacations. John's parents divorced when he was fifteen, and he went to live with his father. His father moved away and John had to leave his friends, including Micah. John now lived more than four hours away from friends he had grown up with. Micah's mother speaks about John's suicide and how it affected her and Micah.

> I think John committed suicide because he no longer could see his friends as often. He was finding it difficult to find work and he felt sort of trapped in a life he didn't want. He was probably depressed. He would visit us maybe once a month and stay for the weekend. The trouble was, I had just taken a new job and was putting in extra hours. I found myself spending all my time working—even most weekends. I think if I had been home more I might have realized that John was depressed and lonely. And, if I'd realized that, I would have arranged for him to live with us and help him find

work. After John's death, Micah went down the tubes. He stopped going to school and was very depressed. This went on for months. I think he blamed himself for John's death. And I was blaming myself for John's death. I finally realized that Micah was depressed so I quit my job. I had a long talk with him and told him that I thought I was responsible for John's death. He cried and told me he thought he was responsible! We both cried. I started spending more time with him and soon he started going back to school. He's in college now and doing well but he almost never talks about John. There's still a loss there that he can't talk about and has never gotten over. I doubt that he ever will. I don't think he lets himself get as close to other friends as he got with John.[16]

Healing After Suicide

There is no easy way to recover from the suicide of a loved one. Some, like Micah's mother and Micah, may never fully recover. However, survivors can do some things that may help ease the pain.

Talking with others is often helpful. Of course, at first a survivor may want or need to withdraw for awhile. Eventually, though, speaking with other family members or friends can help. Some survivors find that talking with good listeners can soften some of the pain, anger, and guilt.[17] These intense emotions are less scary when survivors put words to them and express them to others. Some survivors find speaking with other survivors of suicide helpful.[18] Support groups and organizations for survivors are available in many cities.

Talking about the teenager who died is important. Fond memories are always helpful. Sometimes painful memories may arise, also. It is important to give some thought to

We Got Through This Together

Joe and Julie Cunningham's son Jay shot himself at home shortly before his high school graduation. His parents talk about how they have grieved and tried to recover from his suicide.

Julie: I found his body in the morning. I knew he was dead. I tried to call 911, but I lifted the phone so fast there was no dial tone. Thinking the phone wasn't working, I drove to friends and they called 911. Then I called Joe's school . . . I told the principal and he told Joe. My friends took me back to the house. The police were there. The principal didn't trust Joe to drive himself, so he drove Joe. The first thing Joe said to me was "You know we'll be okay." We have always talked and told each other our feelings. We have never blamed each other.

Joe: We went through a lot of pain, but our friends were always with us through the bad times. They let us talk and always listened to us. . . . Most days, for the last one and a half years, I've driven through the cemetery where Jay is buried. I've found that comforting, being close to him. We were never angry at him or anyone, though I've felt angry at "IT." I'm not sure what "IT" is, though maybe it's the situation.

Julie: We talk about Jay a lot. We tell stories about him and recall places and events that involved him. I spent lots of time trying to piece together why he did it. I went to the library and read about brain chemistry imbalances, impulsivity, and suicide. Eventually there came a time when I didn't need to solve the "why" question. The first of everything was hard—his birthday, the first Christmas without him, the first anniversary of his death. For a while, we both went to a support group for parents whose kids had committed suicide. Our church family and our faith have kept us going.

Joe: At his funeral, the pastor had everyone write some kind of message and put it in this basket. Here's one of the messages: "Jay taught me how to throw one hell of a curve ball." Julie and I read these messages from time to time. Reading them helps us to remember Jay, to laugh and cry, and to heal.[19]

these memories. Keeping them buried or hidden makes grieving more difficult.[20]

Survivors need to take care of themselves during intense grieving. They need to try to get rest and eat at least a little something.[21] Any excess drugs or alcohol during this time will be more harmful than helpful.[22]

At some point, survivors should try to end their attempt to answer the "why" question. They should realize that they will never know for sure why their son or daughter, niece or nephew, grandson or daughter, or friend committed suicide. Their loved one or friend took the reasons to the grave. Survivors can probably piece together some ideas about why the teen committed suicide, but this is probably as close to the real reasons survivors can ever come. Survivors have to face the awful fact that even if they could know the reason, their loved one or friend is not coming back.

The death of a loved one often causes a deep and lasting depression, and other painful emotions. Sometimes this depression increases the risk of suicide in survivors. When these grief reactions are especially strong and do not subside over time, professional help may be needed.[23]

Positive Steps

Whether or not survivors can eventually come to accept the death of a loved one or a close friend, some survivors try to find ways to turn the terrible tragedy into something positive. They have accepted that nothing they can do will bring back their loved one so they look for ways to heal and to help themselves *and* others.

A number of survivors become involved with suicide prevention programs, especially programs that provide education about teen suicide to teens, parents, and other community caregivers. They go to schools, youth centers,

Jay Cunningham, age eighteen, shot himself at home shortly before his high school graduation.

After Les Franklin's son, Shaka, committed suicide at age sixteen, Mr. Franklin quit his job, raised money, and set up a foundation to identify African-American children and teens who might be at risk for suicide.

Shaka Franklin was a talented high school football player (inset).

Les Franklin—Community Activist

Mr. Franklin's sixteen-year-old son, Shaka, committed suicide in 1990. Mr. Franklin has found it very difficult to accept his son's death. However, he realized that he did not want to spend the rest of his life brooding about Shaka's death. He decided that the best way to remember Shaka was to try to help other teens. He quit his job, raised money, and set up a foundation that identifies African-American children and teens who might be at risk for suicide.

My foundation sponsors several programs designed to help children and teens who may be from troubled families, children having trouble in school, or children who have few or no healthy role models to turn to. We feel that if they have positive experiences with people who love them and will help them, their risk for suicide will be lower. There are a lot of kids out there who need this kind of help. We can work twenty-four hours a day and still have kids who need to be reached.[24]

and libraries to talk about teen suicide. Others find ways to develop special outreach programs for children and teens. These programs are often designed to improve teens' self-esteem and coping skills. There are many other ways survivors find to try to reduce teen suicide.

Survivors such as Mr. Franklin work very hard to prevent other teens from committing suicide. These efforts also help them heal from the devastating pain brought on by the suicide of their loved ones.

5

A Look at Prevention

My best friend, Ann, committed suicide a few years ago. She was very depressed. Except for a couple of friends and me, she felt that no one cared about her. She talked about suicide off and on but then she would sound more upbeat. I didn't know what to do. I wish I had known more about suicide then. Maybe I would have made sure she got help. I'd like to become a peer counselor at school. Maybe I can help another teen who's thinking about suicide.

Kelly[1]

Can suicide be prevented? Many suicide experts suggest that many suicides are preventable.[2] However, prevention requires that teens take action.[3] Taking action means participating in existing suicide prevention programs or programs that target high-risk teens or high-risk groups. When prevention programs are unavailable, teens can work with school and community leaders to provide them.

All suicide prevention programs need to be designed and delivered with the help of experts, since a poorly thought-out program can cause negative effects, such as upsetting some student participants.[4]

Studies evaluating the effectiveness of suicide prevention programs are not complete. Preliminary studies show mixed results. Some programs appear slightly more effective than others.[5] In addition, a combination of different programs may offer more success than any single program.[6] Further research in suicide prevention is needed.

School Programs

Since most teenagers attend school, many suicide prevention programs are school-based, and involve educating students and training school staff and peer counselors.

Educating All Students About Suicide

Many schools offer special programs or classes that provide information about suicide. Teachers and special speakers, including teens, raise awareness about the causes, myths, and warning signs of suicide.

Take action: The success of these education programs depends upon teens learning about suicide and its warning signs, and what to do if a friend is suicidal. Teens can get the word out and encourage their friends to attend. Many programs have teen speakers. Volunteer to be a speaker.

Screening Programs to Identify Suicidal Teens

Some schools have developed special questionnaires or interview material and have students fill them out. While this approach is helpful in identifying students who may be thinking about suicide, there are some weaknesses. Since these screening programs are voluntary, not all students are screened. Sometimes the day a teenager is questioned he or she may not be suicidal or thinking about suicide. By the next day the teen may be suicidal.

Take action: While adults (school counselors and psychologists) are usually in charge of these programs, teens can play an important role. They encourage other teens to take part in the screening and make sure they respond to followup efforts. If a teen was helped by a screening program, he or she can share the positive experience with other teens.

Special Programs That Target High-Risk Youth and Suicide Risk Factors

While not specifically suicide prevention programs, programs that target specific suicide risk factors or high-risk youth may help reduce suicide.[7] Since depression and drug and alcohol abuse increase the risk of suicide, programs that help teens with these problems are important. Over half of teens commit suicide with guns so any program that limits access to guns may help.[8] Programs designed to teach coping skills and problem-solving strategies to all teens, as well as teens in crisis, can lower suicide risk.

Take action: Help start an Alcoholics Anonymous teen group. Think of ways to reach depressed teens. There are special programs that teach teens how to solve problems and make good choices. If a school does not offer these classes, ask a principal or teacher about providing them.

Programs Designed to Respond to the Threat of Suicide

It is not enough to educate students and staff or even to identify students who are suicidal. Schools must respond to students who are suicidal. Many schools work with experts and the local community to develop ways to deal with suicidal students. Some schools develop special suicide response teams as well as good referral resources in the community for these teens.

Take action: If there is no directory of resources in the community that deals with suicidal youth, meet with school and community leaders to develop one. Apply for funds or find a sponsor who will print this directory. Find ways to distribute this directory to all teens in the community.

Peer Counseling and Support Groups

Some peer counseling and support programs may help students reduce high-risk behaviors associated with suicide.[9] Student volunteers are trained in peer counseling techniques, and are supervised by school psychologists or counselors. Since teens with problems are often reluctant to talk about their problems with adults, peer counseling programs are effective ways to reach students.

Take action: Teens should encourage their schools to have peer counseling or peer support groups, or help get such programs started. Be a peer counselor. Peer counselors need to have good listening skills and other training to do this sensitive and difficult work. Well-run peer counseling programs train and supervise the peer counselor.

There are many other ways schools help prevent teen suicide besides having specific suicide prevention programs or programs that target high-risk students. The atmosphere of a school can contribute to a positive learning and social environment as well as help prevent high-risk behaviors. Building smaller schools and having smaller classes is a frequent suggestion. Other proposals include the following:

1. Establishing community schools in tune with the needs and problems of the neighborhoods.

2. Organizing schools in ways that encourage school staff to function as team members.

3. Promoting expanded roles for teachers.

4. Creating alternative schools that truly address the special needs of their students.[10]

Other Programs

Not all teens are in school. Some have dropped out; others have graduated. So communities need to develop programs outside of schools.

Special Community Resources and Programs

Many communities have organizations, hospitals, and agencies that offer special programs for suicidal youth, programs for high-risk individuals and groups, and suicide prevention. These organizations include local hospitals, mental health centers, mental health associations, YMCAs, and local sports teams. Some community programs are started by survivors of suicide. Check to see what programs are available in the community.

Take action: Darlene and Dale Emme lost their son to suicide. They began a program that involves the distribution of Yellow Ribbon cards. A suicidal teen hands this card to a friend or an adult. The card has printed on it: "This card is a cry for help. Stay with the person. You are their lifeline. They may not be able to tell you their needs if they are in severe emotional pain or distress. Get them to, or call someone who can help, if you cannot!" Many teens have used this card to get help for themselves. Help the Emmes distribute this card to other young people. (See "For More Information.")

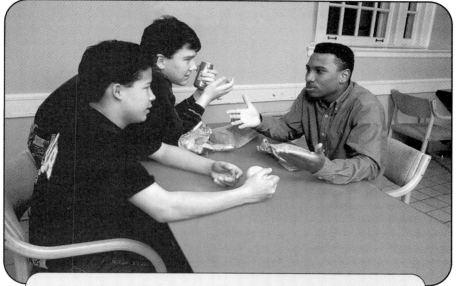

Peer counseling and support groups may help students reduce high-risk behaviors associated with suicide.

Suicide Hot Lines and Crisis Centers

Many communities offer suicide hot lines or crisis centers. Suicide hot lines are usually staffed either by trained volunteers or professional counselors. Hot lines operate twenty-four hours a day and their services are free. Privacy is important, so a person does not have to identify himself or herself. The staff is trained to handle the suicidal caller, who is usually, though not always, in a crisis. The suicidal person is encouraged to talk about the situation or issues that cause him or her to feel suicidal. When the caller seems less suicidal because he seems calmer, he may be given the names of counselors or centers to go to for follow-up.

Take action: If a community does not have a teen hot line or crisis center, help set one up. If there is one, volunteer. The training is rigorous. Being a hot line volunteer is hard work and requires commitment and dedication.

Though it is important for schools and communities to develop suicide prevention programs, it is equally important to spread the word about these programs and to make access and referral to some of the specialized programs easy and free. Some school districts and other community agencies have arranged for suicidal teens to receive short-term counseling sessions free.

Most people who attempt suicide and whose attempts are prevented are grateful for being saved.[11] More people need to learn about suicide and get involved. Teens need to take action, help each other, and participate in programs that seek to prevent teen suicide. The prevention of teen suicide is a worthy and achievable goal!

Afterword

Consider what the world would have been like without Albert Einstein, Abraham Lincoln, Martin Luther King, Jr., Pablo Picasso, or Eleanor Roosevelt. What if they had committed suicide when they were teenagers? Their unique contributions to our lives would be lost.

John, Shaka, Jay, and Ann all took their own lives when they were very young. Their families and friends can only wonder what they might have grown up to be and what contributions they may have made to their communities and to the world had they lived.

They can only wonder and weep.

For More Information

American Association of Suicidology
4201 Connecticut Avenue, NW
Suite 310
Washington, DC 20008
(202) 237-2280
<http://www.suicidology.org>

Centers for Disease Control and Prevention
Atlanta, Georgia
<http://www.cdc.gov>

National Institute of Mental Health
NIMH Public Inquiries
6001 Executive Blvd., Rm. 8184
MSC 9663
Bethesda, MD 20892-9663
(301) 443-4513
<http://www.nimh.nih.gov>

National Suicide Hot Line (24 hours)
(Ask for a local suicide hot-line number.)
(800) 555-1212

Local Suicide Hot Lines
Look in the phone book under
    Suicide hot line
    Suicide crisis center

Light for Life Foundation
An organization that helps suicidal youth.
Send for ten free yellow ribbon cards and for other information.
(303) 429-3530
<http://www.yellowribbon.org>

**Handgun Control and the Center to Prevent
Handgun Violence**
1225 Eye Street NW, Suite 1100
Washington, D.C. 20005
(202) 898-0792
<http://www.cphv.org>

Pride for Youth
Peer Counseling for Gay Youth
(516) 679-9000
<http://www.licrisiscenter.org/pride.html>

Finding other Internet sources

Use several search engines such as Yahoo and Lycos as follows:

Type in words or phrases such as *suicide, teen suicide, youth suicide.*

Chapter Notes

Chapter 1. Overview of Suicide

1. Personal interview with Sharon (not her real name), September 10, 1998.

2. Centers for Disease Control (CDC), Suicide Deaths and Rates Per 100,000 (1995) (Atlanta: Centers for Disease Control), n.d. <http://www.cdc.gov/ncipc/osp/us9592/suic.htm> (May 6, 1999).

3. Ibid.

4. Alan L. Berman and David A. Jobes, "Suicide Prevention in Adolescents (Age 12–18)," *Suicide and Life-Threatening Behavior* 25, no. 1, Spring 1995, p. 143.

5. David Lester, *Making Sense of Suicide: An In-Depth Look at Why People Kill Themselves* (Phila.: The Charles Press, 1997), pp. 6–8.

6. George Howe Colt, *The Enigma of Suicide* (New York: Summit Books, 1991), p. 39.

7. Centers for Disease Control, 1997 Youth Risk Behavior Surveillance System (YRBSS) (Atlanta: Centers for Disease Control, 1997) <http://www.cdc.gov/nccdphp/dash/yrbs/natsum97/susu97.htm> (May 6, 1999).

8. Centers for Disease Control, Suicide Deaths and Rates Per 100,000 (1995).

9. Lester, pp. 100–101.

10. Centers for Disease Control, 1997 Youth Risk Behavior Surveillance System.

11. Paul R. Robbins, *Adolescent Suicide* (Jefferson, N.C.: McFarland & Company, Inc., 1998), p. 11.

12. Ronald Maris, "The Adolescent Suicide Problem," *Suicide and Life-Threatening Behavior* 15, no. 2, Summer 1985, pp. 97–99.

13. Lester, p. 12.

14. Ibid., p. v.

15. Brent Q. Hafen and Kathryn J. Frandsen, *Youth Suicide: Depression and Loneliness* (Evergreen, Colo.: Cordillera Press, Inc., 1986), p. 10.

16. Centers for Disease Control, Suicide Deaths and Rates Per 100,000 (1995).

17. Ibid.

18. Ibid.

19. Ibid.

20. Arlene Metha, Barbara Weber, and L. Dean Webb, "Youth Suicide Prevention: A Survey and Analysis of Policies and Efforts in the 50 States," Table 1, *Suicide and Life-Threatening Behavior* 28, no. 2, Summer 1998, p. 151.

21. Centers for Disease Control, 1997 Youth Risk Behavior Surveillance System.

22. Lester, pp. 107–109.

23. Robert Garofalo, et al, "Sexual Orientation and Risk of Suicide Attempts Among a Representative Sample of Youth," *Archives of Pediatrics and Adolescent Medicine*, vol. 153, May 1999, p. 487.

24. David Lester, *The Cruelest Death: The Enigma of Adolescent Suicide* (Phila.: The Charles Press, 1993), pp. vii–viii.

25. National Mental Health Association, *Teen Depression and Suicide* pamphlet (Alexandria, Va.: National Mental Health Association, November 1998).

26. Hafen and Frandsen, p. 17.

27. Lester, *The Cruelest Death*, pp. vii–viii.

28. Madelyn S. Gould, David Shaffer, and Marjorie Kleinman, "The Impact of Suicide in Television Movies: Replication and Commentary," *Suicide and Life-Threatening Behavior* 18, no. 1, Spring 1998, pp. 97–98.

29. Lester, *Making Sense of Suicide*, pp. 147–149.

30. Robbins, pp. 129–130.

31. Centers for Disease Control, *Youth Suicide Prevention Programs: A Resource Guide*, Table 8 (Atlanta: Centers for Disease Control, 1992), p. 148.

32. Arthur Kellerman, et al., "Suicide in the Home in Relation to Gun Ownership," *The New England Journal of Medicine* 327, no. 7, 1992, p. 467.

33. Centers for Disease Control, *Youth Suicide Prevention Programs: A Resource Guide*, Table 8, p. 148.

34. Robbins, pp. 66–67.

35. Hafen and Frandsen, pp. 144–145.

Chapter 2. Why Teens Commit Suicide
1. Personal interview with Sharon, September 10, 1998.

2. Paul R. Robbins, *Adolescent Suicide* (Jefferson, N.C.: McFarland & Company, Inc., 1998), pp. 91–95.

3. Ibid., pp. 60–62.

4. Ibid., pp. 62–63.

5. Andrew Slaby and Lili Frank Garfinkel, *No One Saw My Pain: Why Teens Kill Themselves* (New York: W. W. Norton & Company, 1996), pp. 5–6, 127, 136, 141.

6. National Mental Health Association, *Depression: What You Need to Know* pamphlet (Alexandria, Va.: National Mental Health Association, n.d.).

7. Ibid.

8. American Psychiatric Association, *Diagnostic and Statistical Manual of Mental Disorders—Fourth Edition* (Washington, D.C.: American Psychiatric Association, 1994), p. 327.

9. Brent Q. Hafen and Kathryn J. Frandsen, *Youth Suicide: Depression and Loneliness* (Evergreen, Colo.: Cordillera Press, Inc., 1986), p. 147.

10. Interview with Sharon.

11. David A. Brent, et al., "Risk Factors for Adolescent Suicide," *Archives of General Psychiatry* 45, June 1988, p. 584.

12. Personal interview with Stan (not his real name), May 3, 1998.

13. Robbins, pp. 65–66.

14. Ibid., pp. 80–84.

15. David Lester, *The Cruelest Death: The Enigma of Adolescent Suicide* (Phila.: The Charles Press, 1993), pp. 99–100.

16. Richard Jessor, "Risk Behavior in Adolescence: A Psychosocial Framework for Understanding and Action," *Journal of Adolescent Health* 12, no. 8, 1991, p. 602.

17. Washington State Department of Health, *Youth Suicide Prevention Plan for Washington State* (Olympia: Washington State Department of Health, January 1995), p. 15.

Chapter 3. Helping a Suicidal Friend

1. Personal interview with Debbie, May 10, 1998.

2. Carey Goldberg with Marjone Connelly, "Poll Finds Decline in Teen-Age Fear and Violence," *The New York Times*, October 20, 1999, pp. A1, A22.

3. Brent Q. Hafen and Kathryn J. Frandsen, *Youth Suicide: Depression and Loneliness* (Evergreen, Colo.: Cordillera Press, Inc., 1986), p. 19.

4. Ibid., p. 140.

5. Paul R. Robbins, *Adolescent Suicide* (Jefferson, N.C.: McFarland & Company, Inc., 1998), pp. 62–63.

6. David A. Brent, et al., "Risk Factors for Adolescent Suicide," *Archives of General Psychiatry* 45, June 1988, p. 585.

7. Hafen and Frandsen, pp. 116–131.

8. Personal interview with Joe and Julie Cunningham, August 6, 1998.

9. Lester, pp. 167–170.

Chapter 4. Surviving Suicide

1. Personal interview with Les Franklin, June 25, 1998.

2. Earl A. Grollman, *Straight Talk about Death for Teenagers: How to Cope with Losing Someone You Love* (Boston: Beacon Press, 1993), pp. 12–13.

3. Ibid., p. 11.

4. Andrew Slaby and Lili Frank Garfinkel, *No One Saw My Pain: Why Teens Kill Themselves* (New York: W. W. Norton & Company, 1996), p. 167.

5. Ibid., p. 28.

6. David Lester, *Making Sense of Suicide: An In-Depth Look at Why People Kill Themselves* (Philadelphia: The Charles Press, 1997), p. 180.

7. Ibid., p. 181.

8. Ibid.

9. Ibid.

10. National Mental Health Association, *Coping with Loss*, pamphlet (Alexandria, Va.: National Mental Health Association, January 5, 1999).

11. Lester, p. 181.

12. Personal interview with Kelly (not her real name), March 16, 1998.

13. Lester, p. 180.

14. David Lester, *The Cruelest Death: The Enigma of Adolescent Suicide* (Phila.: The Charles Press, 1993), p. 144.

15. Lester, *Making Sense of Suicide*, p. 181.

16. Personal interview with Carol, July 18, 1998.

17. Earl A. Grollman, *Straight Talk About Death for Teenagers: How to Cope with Losing Someone You Love* (Boston: Beacon Press, 1993), pp. 101–103.

18. Lester, *Making Sense of Suicide*, p. 181.

19. Personal interview with Joe and Julie Cunningham, August 6, 1998.

20. Catherine M. Sanders, *How to Survive the Loss of a Child: Filling the Emptiness and Rebuilding Your Life* (Rocklin, Calif.: Prima Publishing, 1992), p. 115.

21. National Mental Health Association, *Coping with Loss*.

22. Grollman, pp. 96–97.

23. Lester, *Making Sense of Suicide*, p. 181.

24. Interview with Les Franklin.

Chapter 5. A Look at Prevention

1. Personal interview with Kelly (not her real name), March 16, 1998.

2. David Lester, *Making Sense of Suicide: An In-Depth Look at Why People Kill Themselves* (Phila.: The Charles Press, 1997), pp. viii–ix.

3. Brent Q. Hafen and Kathryn J. Frandsen, *Youth Suicide: Depression and Loneliness* (Evergreen, Colo.: Cordillera Press, Inc., 1986), pp. 19–20.

4. Centers for Disease Control, *Youth Suicide Prevention Programs: A Resource Guide* (Atlanta: Centers for Disease Control, 1992), p. 67.

5. Jenny Ploeg, et al., "A Systematic Overview of Adolescent Suicide Prevention Programs," *Canadian Journal of Public Health* 25, no. 5, September–October 1996, p. 320.

6. Paul R. Robbins, *Adolescent Suicide* (Jefferson, N.C.: McFarland & Company, Inc., 1998), p. 130.

7. Arlene Metha, Barbara Weber, and L. Dean Webb, "Youth Suicide Prevention: A Survey and Analysis of Policies and Efforts in the 50 States," *Suicide and Life-Threatening Behavior* 28, no. 2, Summer 1998, p. 163.

8. Lester, pp. 181–183.

9. Centers for Disease Control, *Youth Suicide Prevention Programs: A Resource Guide*, p. 116.

10. Joy G. Dryfoos, "Adolescents at Risk: A Summation of Work in the Field—Programs and Policies," *Journal of Adolescent Health* 12, 1991, pp. 630–637.

11. Lester, p. 183.

Glossary

alcohol abuse—Drinking excessive amounts of alcohol, usually to the point of intoxication and impaired functioning.

ambivalence—When a person cannot decide whether to do something, such as commit suicide.

brain chemistry—Various chemicals in the brain that are required for normal mental and physical functioning.

cluster suicides—Shortly after one teen commits suicide, several other teens also commit suicide, often using the same or similar methods. Also called *copycat* suicides.

crisis—A situation requiring immediate action or intervention.

crisis center—A place where a person in crisis can call or go and speak with a trained counselor.

depression—An emotional illness that causes a person to have feelings of sadness and hopelessness, and to have difficulty functioning over a long period.

drug abuse—The excessive use of either prescription drugs or illegal drugs that often causes impaired functioning and uninhibited behavior.

grief—Intense feelings of sadness or sorrow usually following a loss or death.

guilt—Feelings of self-blame.

hot lines—Services reached by phone where trained staff are available to talk about problems or crises.

humiliation—A feeling of hurt pride or public embarrassment.

myth—A common belief people may have that is not true.

shame—A painful feeling associated with bad behavior.

suicide—The act of killing oneself.

suicide rates—The number of suicides per every 100,000 people. This figure is usually calculated by groups, for example, the suicide rate for white males (all ages) was 21.4 in 1995.

survivor—The person who is left after a loved one or close friend commits suicide.

Further Reading

Axelrod, Toby. *Working Together Against Teen Suicide*. New York: The Rosen Publishing Group, 1996.

Crook, Marion. *Suicide: Teens Talk to Teens*. Bellingham, Wash.: Self-Counsel Press, 1997.

Grollman, Earl A. *Straight Talk About Death for Teenagers: How to Cope With Losing Someone You Love*. Boston: Beacon Press, 1993.

Kuklin, Susan. *After a Suicide: Young People Speak Up*. New York: Putnam, 1994.

Nelson, Richard E., and Judith C. Galas. *The Power to Prevent Suicide*. Minneapolis: Free Spirit, 1994.

Slaby, Andrew, and Lili Frank Garfinkel. *No One Saw My Pain. Why Teens Kill Themselves*. New York: W. W. Norton & Company, Inc., 1994.

Internet Sites

American Foundation for Suicide Prevention
<http://www.afsp.org>

The Compassionate Friends
<http://www.compassionatefriends.org>

National Mental Health Association
<http://www.nmha.org>

San Francisco Suicide Prevention
<http://www.sfsuicide.org>

Index

A
abuse
  alcohol and drug, 8, 13,
    19–21, 26–27
  emotional, 16
  physical, 16
  sexual, 16
anger, 33–34

B
behavior
  aggressive, 15
  changes in, 15, 27
  dangerous, 20, 21, 26
  high-risk, 47, 49
brain chemistry, 14–15

C
crisis centers, 49
counseling
  peer, 45, 47
  professional, 16, 30

D
depression, 8, 13–16
  causes of, 14–15
  signs of, 15
  treatment, 16
death
  accidental, 7, 20
  causes of, 7–8
  dealing with, 38–40, 43
  unclear case of, 7–8

distortions, 14
divorce, 16, 19
drugs, 13

F
family
  breakdown or disturbance,
    8, 13, 16, 19, 26
friend
  confiding in, 26
  helping a, 28–30, 31

G
grief
  difficulties of, 32–40
  features of, 33–36
  survivor, 36–37
guilt, 34–35, 37
  survivor, 34–35, 38
guns, 11, 31, 46

H
high-risk teens, 44, 46
hopelessness, 13–15, 26
hot lines, 30, 49–50

L
listening, 30, 38

M
media and suicide, 8, 9